LOS

RISE
AND
FALL

DRABBLES CONCERNING THE
BIRTH AND DEATHS OF CIVILIZATIONS

First Edition
Published by
Nordic Press
Kindlyckevägen 13
Rimforsa, Sweden.
2022
This is a work of fiction. Similarities to real people, places, or events are entirely coincidental.
Rise and Fall
978-91-987509-1-1
Cover Design, Edited and Compiled by
David Green
Formatted by
C. Marry Hultman
Copyright © 2022 Nordic Press

EMPIRES

UNTOLD STORIES·	8
GONE AND FORGOTTEN·	9
THE ROYAL ARTHURIANS·	10
POMPEII·	11
RETURN OF THE OLD ONES·	12
ALONE·	13
AND ON EARTH WITHOUT CHANGES·	14
THE FALL OF THE MINOANS·	15
OPEN THE FLOODGATES·	16
FINAL SWING·	17
KING FOR A DAY·	18
PIZARRO VISITS THE INCA·	19
THE FROG KINGDOM AND COMET GAMMA 9·	20
CLEOPATRA·	21
THE FALL OF THE MOTHER KING·	22
THE DARKNESS·	23
SACRIFICE·	24
OUT OF THE FRYING PAN·	25
RESOLVE·	26
PROGRESS·	27
BIRTH OF THE MOUNTAIN-VALLEY NATION·	28
A LOOK TO THE SKY·	29
THE PLUTO CRYSTALS·	30
WAR HORSE·	31
THE LAST DAYS OF DARLENIA·	32
THE REASON FOR COLLAPSE·	33
AGAINST THE GRAIN·	34
APACHES TO ALDEBARAN·	35

The Shield of Gaia·	36
The End of Hunger·	37
The Wave·	38
The First Dark Soul·	39
Library Nation·	40
All Hail the Clowns·	41
A Matter of Darkness·	42
A Conscious Decision·	43
No Escape·	44
Tashima District·	45
There Goes the Neighborhood·	46
The Serpent·	47
From Verona With Love·	48
Mean Girls·	49
My Master's Friend, Forever·	50
The New Gods·	51
Something was Wrong·	52
Last Day of Pompeii·	53
The Drowned Village·	54
A Case For Kay·	55
Desolate·	56
The Sock·	57
Unfinished Paintings·	58
Once the Largest City in North America·	
	59
Shrouded Vengeance·	60
Little Dog Alone·	61
The Blossoming·	62
The Clan·	63
Blood of the Enemy·	64
Museum of Rarities·	65

Foundations of Empire·	66
Matilda's Final Day·	67
Pollution·	68
Great Men·	69
Temperalis·	70
Fire and Ash·	71
Lives Forever Changed ·	72
Gone to the Dogs·	73
The Do-Over·	74
The God of Time·	75
Evolution ·	76
Home Sweet Home·	77
An off the record addition to the Conclusions of the Intergalactic Investigations Committee.·	78
The Ultimate Equation·	79
A Final Visit With Billy Lee·	80
Death's Blessing·	81
Ashes·	82
A Vanished Culture·	83
Completed·	84
Space Race·	85
The Romanovs·	86
Wipe Out·	87
Bombs Away·	88
The Ashes of Troy·	89
The Old Gods·	90
All Hail The Queen·	91
When they Discarded Inhumanity·	92
Into The Depths·	93
This Song Goes Out to You ·	94

IN THIS LIGHT·	95
ROME'S SUNSET WILL RISE·	96
MEDUSA AND ATHENA·	97
WORLD PEACE·	98
AMBITION·	99
KARL I, THE LAST EMPEROR·	100
THE SHAKERS·	101
THE LAND OF KINGS·	102
NO RIDES BACK·	103
DEATH OF AN ARMY·	104
THE PLANET'S FURY·	105
THE SILENCE OF CATTLE·	106
DOGTOPIA·	107
THE JOKE·	108
THE SCULPTOR·	109
FIRST CONTACT·	110
THE WINTER WARMING·	111
HOMECOMING·	112
MOTHER KNOWS BEST·	113
SCAPEGOAT·	114
THE RIVER·	115
THE SWEET LIFE·	116
ACCIDENTAL EXTINCTION·	117
MEGA CHURCH·	118
THE CITY AT THE END OF THE WORLD·	119
MURDEROUS EYES·	120
CHILDREN OF THE MIGHTY DOLLAR·	121
COME TO PASS·	122
CALCIUM STARVED·	123
PAST MISTAKES·	124
A VIEW FROM THE SEA·	125

UNTOLD STORIES

Ximena Escobar

One drop of crystalline water.
And in that drop, the whole world.
Within that world, a multitude of windows.
Within each window, a million soulful eyes.

I opened my hand, knelt on the blackness. Stretched my palm, let it slide onto the nothing. Watched it float, separate into alien-like fingers, reaching for something—but the nothing solidified.

The hand evaporated.

I had to tell myself, "I'm afraid we're alone in the universe."

Watching it glide away like a nebula, I learned galaxies had been but blind spots.

We'd been no more than a miracle.

And nobody else would see it.

Gone And Forgotten

Jade Wildy

The archeostorian laboured over the archives, drawing out entries to be cleaned and clarified and spat out for review. There were quadrillions of entries, and a flotilla of archeostorians carefully catalogued them all.

"The human race..." this one began, and the archeostorian watched a recount of the civilization's greatest achievements.

Revolt followed art. War followed technology. Exploration followed revolution for thousands of years.

Curious about this strange race, the archeostorian ran the term 'humans' through the database.

No other entries.

Whoever they were, these humans were now long gone. Their insignificant civilization didn't even gain a footnote in Galactic history.

The Royal Arthurians

Abdul-Qaadir Taariq Bakari-Muhammad

"When darkness fell from the four corners of the world, my brethren soon rejoiced in freedom. And yet, this plagued me with saddened heart. A moment of jubilee should never suffice under the yoke of false superiority. The walking skyscrapers have fallen, and we shall rightfully take their place. It soothes me to see their ashes wither next to our droppings. No more cramped crevices. We seek kingdoms spread throughout the world as far as our eyes can see. The destiny of man finally replaced by the Blattodea of the Arthurians. May their skulls become the bedrock of our roundtables

Pompeii

Nat Whiston

The room shakes as we huddle in the corner of the temple, praying, vases crash, and pillars fall to the ground. My daughter sobs into my toga as I wonder what we could have done to displease the gods. Screams echo around us as Mount Vesuvius erupts. I tell my wife to pray harder as the people run from the sanctuary. A carpet of fire comes towards the entrance, and the building begins to crumble; I fear the gods have forsaken us. I kiss my daughter on the head and hope that we will all be reunited in the afterlife.

Return of the Old Ones

Wondra Vanian

There were things on this planet long before the sludge that became humankind clambered up onto two legs—and they weren't happy with what had become of their home since then.

Scattered, confused reports claimed giants had risen from inside mountain ranges and below desert sands. Anything built atop them while they slept crumbled away as they shook themselves awake.

The more woke humans blamed climate change when the earth shook, but their self-righteous indignation didn't save them any more than the thoughts and prayers of their less educated counterparts.

When the Old Ones rose again, humanity fell as one.

Alone

Scarlett Lake

The vastness of space is incomprehensible until you're alone within its cold empty grasp. For five years, Quinn has been searching. Before her there was another. He only lasted two years before he locked himself into one of the docking bays and jettisoned the air, blasting himself into the universe.

Simon was just one in a long line of failed saviours, number 99 of 100 chosen. Quinn knows it's down to her, that she is the last one left, the last designated survivor of the human race. The last one with the training. The last to search the cosmos; alone.

AND ON EARTH WITHOUT CHANGES

Christopher T. Drabrowski

There is no point in visiting the Earth.

Nobody would want to live there. It would be a guarantee of rapid health loss and even death.

Holidays? Yes, it used to be beautiful in some places. But now it is a thing of the past.

Only robots are left there, exploiting the planet's natural resources. Only they can survive there.

Even the technicians have eschewed maintenance visits, programming them to check and repair themselves when necessary.

And only occasionally, school trips from colonised planets arrive to teach kids from an early age how to take care of their own planets.

The Fall of the Minoans

Claire Davon

It all started with the tsunami. Then the cold summers and ruined crops. Their seers speculated that the volcano that erupted on Thera may have caused this, but they could not prove it to the king. That island, a major trading partner, had been destroyed. These disasters made the people lose faith in the priest kings of the formerly great Minoan civilization, leading to this.

His greatest failure.

He had lost.

As the king stood in front of the Greek invaders, his head bowed in surrender, he understood their time was over. The Minoans and their culture were no more.

Open the Floodgates

McKenzie Richardson

The sea swept through the floodgates, toppling the island like a ship giving in to the storm.

Elin fought against the waves. The mass of bodies pressed against hers as the waters rose.

White-gold eyes lit the shadows, housed in a face as green as moss. Emerald lips brushed hers. A breath of life caressed her tongue and slithered down her throat as her lungs filled.

Then the morgen pulled Elin to join the other newly converted islanders in a swirling dance of flashing fins.

Some say that was the end of Cantre'r Gwaelod.

But that was when it truly began

FINAL SWING

Radar DeBoard

Arterious had trained his whole life for one moment, and he was not going to fail as the time came. So even though his muscles ached, and he was covered in the wounds of battle, Aterious pushed himself through the chaos. His movements were so fluid that the sorcerer didn't even see Atreious until it was far too late.

There was no hesitation from the young man as he swung his sword, separating the tyrannical magic wielder's head from its body. It took but one swing of a sword for an empire to fall, while a new one rose forth.

KING FOR A DAY

NICK JOHNSON

A child wrapped in bejewelled robes was, for the first time in his life, washed, bathed, and fed. Just the day before, the boy lived on the streets, but today he was a king! The duration in paradise was brief, though.

As the sun fell, the pauper turned prince, his belly full of lamb, his skin covered in silk, and his head crowned in gold was laid down on an altar and gutted by a high priest who begged deaf gods to bring rain while yesterday's king quietly took back his crown and placed it upon his own head again.

Pizarro Visits the Inca

John Mueter

Who are these strange bearded men who appeared from another world, brutal, merciless, whose armour glistens in the sun, whose weapons cut us to shreds, whose short spears spray fire into us? What are these creatures they ride, bigger than four llamas, that rear up and trample us under their hooves? AYI!

I hid behind a pillar, watching their deadly work. The Sapa Inca Atahualpa, god-on-earth, is thrown from his palanquin, stripped of his robes, rolls naked in the dust. My people flee in terror. AYI!

The whole world is disintegrating! Help us, Inte, who holds the sky!

The Frog Kingdom and Comet Gamma 9

Bryan White

About a million years ago, the frogs of Earth were irradiated by a passing comet. No other creatures in this ancient period were affected.

Within a small pond in the middle of present-day Africa, a special frog declared to all frogs telepathically that she was the queen of the bogs and swamps. A frog on the Southern Pangaean tip discovered fire. Frogs were on their way, but when the comet swung by Earth again, the tiny wheels, huts, axes, and saddles for rats were useless. The queen was eaten by a gigantic asp.

The smartest frogs just wanted flies.

Cleopatra

John Mueter

I've had a bad run of it, betting on the wrong horse every time. But this girl ain't done yet! I hoped Julius Caesar would be my ticket, but he gets himself turned into a human pin cushion in the Roman Senate House. And Mark Antony—big loser! He couldn't win a battle if he were fighting drunken chimpanzees. He screws up big time at Actium and then offs himself. So here I am, left holding the bag. But I'm escaping to India, will get myself together and I'll be back.

Now who let that damn asp loose again . . .
OUCH!

The Fall of The Mother King

Deborah Dubas Groom

The carrion eaters shrieked as they spiralled down to scavenge the corpses. A bitter smile twisted Nefertiti's lips. These would-be assassins had once bowed before her, the co-regent of Akhenaten. She warned her husband that the priests would not submit to the worship of the one god. When her image replaced the goddesses, their kohl-lined eyes filled with murder.

Eight years later, all records of her ceased. Now, hiding in the desert shadows, her famous beauty weathered in the heat, she bowed to the inevitable.

Aten, the sun god, and she, the mother king, would become dust.

The Darkness

Destiny Eve Pifer

High above on the rocky mountain overlooking the small village, the two lovers met.

Embracing one another, they held on, knowing that soon it would all be over. In the distance, they could hear the rumble as those below frantically ran towards their horses. Men, women, and children cried out as the rumbling came closer.

The lovers could only look on in horror as a cloud of darkness seeped through every crack and devoured each one. There was no place to hide. The darkness was far too clever.

They held each other close as it engulfed them. Leaving nothing behind.

Sacrifice

Emma K. Leadley

The Dorset nomadic people travelled in small tribes, greeting their kin with open arms should they meet.

Except for one group.

This sect knew dark magic: rather than creating the humble, protective adornments of their people, they carved ivory and bone into grotesqueries, using them as hunting amulets. And when they killed, it was with abandoned glee, hacking and slashing in synchrony, screaming and smearing themselves and each other in the warm, sticky blood of their prey.

And once a year they made the ultimate sacrifice, stealing a child under moonlit sky, for that child never to be seen again.

Out of the Frying Pan

John H. Dromey

Petros was a rolling stone in his youth. Later, he abandoned his nomadic life to settle in Mesopotamia and take up farming. In effect, he traded sore feet—from routinely crossing the burning sand of deserts—for an all-too-often aching back from tending crops.

Although silt from the Tigris and the Euphrates beneficially enriched the soil, those two rivers could also bring destruction.

Following a massive flood, Petros was nowhere to be found.

"Did he drown?" a neighbour wondered.

"No," another replied. "Fed up with having his fields under water, he packed his belongings and left."

"Where'd he go?"

"Atlantis."

RESOLVE

Radar DeBoard

Nyolite had spent decades climbing her way up the military ranks, and once she was on top, all she had to do was wait. The man who had been ruling over their empire was a clueless dictator, and it did not take long for the people to rebel.

Nyolite seized the opportunity and moved to strike down the Emperor and take control. There was but one true obstacle standing in her way. Nyolite's son was head of the royal guard, and all believed she would not strike him down. Nyolite proved them all wrong by taking her own son's head.

Progress

McKenzie Richardson

The ocean was blue once, like rippling sapphires. I stare out at the tides, now grey and choked.

In my youth, I raced those waves, frolicked through greenery with the other satyrs. Our fur was soft, our bellies full, unlike the tattered half-starved creatures we've become.

They found Pan's body in the meadow this morning, filled with the plastic scraps he'd tried to coax nourishment from.

Our god is dead. There's no hope left for this island.

As the sun sets on Arcadia, it rises on the smog-coated world the humans created in the name of what they deem progress.

Birth of the Mountain-Valley Nation

Shawn M. Klimek

On the battlefield between their facing armies, the mountain and valley kings conferred beneath a white flag.

"Our ancestors were brothers," said the valley king. "Yet we have battled each other for generations. Now, foreign enemies amass their armies on our borders. I suggest it's time we finally unite as a single nation."

"Wisely said," agreed the mountain king. "But which of us should lead this new nation?"

"You are the greater warrior," acknowledged the valley king. "But the leader of our nation must be the wisest of us."

"In that case," said the mountain king. "I accept your surrender."

A Look to the Sky

Stephen Johnson

Huddled in the corner, Boga shakes as violent red sand and rocks pound the inside of the abandoned cavern. What's left of his once noble tribe stares back towards him. Desperate and defeated faces show the shock of the collapse of the village after the fires from the sky destroyed everything.

Boga rises slowly, realising he must now lead the tribe. So many are gone, he laments. He turns to peer out into the dark night sky, longing for the peace he finds in the familiar blue planet that he watches each evening. Always wondering, is there life there too?

The Pluto Crystals

Bryan White

They whizzed over and never stopped. The nerve.

We crystals don't move too fast and don't do much, but we are highly offended. They come from the third bright dot around our God star. We can't imagine how hot it must be there.

Well, we have plans for them.

We want to show them the crystal way. We can move giant rocks floating in the black void with our crystal forces. We sent an extra special big rock to that third blue dot. We calculate if we nudge them a little with our rocks, they will stop and say hello.

War Horse

Emma K. Leadley

Thirty men sat silently in the cramped, dark space. Their thighs pressed against those of their neighbours' and it smelled of stale sweat and piss, with no respite.

A jerk aroused them from their stupor.

Hours of lurching movement followed and when it stopped, a huge cheer sounded outside. Later, in silence, with swords readied, the Greeks disembarked their wooden horse and took in grateful lungfuls of fresh night air. They overcame the drunken Trojans, slitting the throats of their greatest warriors. And high on the adrenaline rush of victory, they slaughtered fleeing families and razed Troy to the ground.

The Last Days of Darlenia

Andrew Kurtz

The skies darkened over the cities of Darlenia as the alien ships hovered above.

"The Darlenians have beautiful sculptures depicting their numerous gods, pure green flora in the parks, stores packed with citizens purchasing goods and buildings constructed of the finest material.

"Burn it all down!" the alien commander ordered his troops as green death rays emerged from the ships.

The statues were reduced to rubble, flora was consumed in flames, turning the green leaves to charcoal black, stores and buildings exploded on impact and flaming corpses littered the streets.

The ships departed the planet to destroy another flourishing civilization.

THE REASON FOR COLLAPSE

Radar DeBoard

Millenia had passed since the Obwaha empire had mysteriously fallen, and scholars had no answers to what caused the demise. Many ambitious archaeologists searched their burial sites, hoping to find insight and stake their claim to academic glory.

It took several years, but a group of college students finally discovered what had happened to the Obwaha. Their empire had been decimated by another, the Lanacans, or as they were most well-known as the spider people. The college students had stumbled across the Lanacans' place of rest, awakening them and unintentionally bringing them forth to begin a new reign of terror.

Against the Grain

T.L. Beeding

"Well, would you look at that?"

Michael gazed into Metatron's looking glass, observing the industrious scene inside. He had to admit he was impressed; things seemed to be going very well, despite the Creator's misgivings. Humanity was constantly advancing to new heights, gaining new knowledge. Bettering themselves in ways he could never have imagined.

And it was all thanks to his brother.

"Good for him," Michael nodded, stroking his chin. Keeping his voice low, to avoid the Creator's over-attentive ears. "I'm happy things worked in his favour."

Metatron chuckled. "Lucifer always did have a soft spot for humans, didn't he?"

Apaches to Aldebaran

Bryan White

Rome may have been built in a day, but it was destroyed in two seconds.

Quite by luck, the Apache Nation of North America developed a device that could convert air into fire. A hundred years after the Colonists were defeated, the Apaches ruled the continent, travelled to the moon, and harnessed the atom.

Across the ocean, the Kingdom of Italy had done about the same. Europe was their playground and breadbasket. Rome and the Apaches never liked each other though, and the Apaches wrecked Rome Pompeii volcano style.

Freed of conflict, the Apaches travelled to the stars shortly after.

The Shield of Gaia

Rho Mack

When our first-gens were in lockdown before the escape launch from super-heated Earth, there were rumours of an alternate team, one of them fake.

The rush on the launch control room was legendary, our creation myth: cut communication during liftoff, no further supply payloads. We never heard how it ended down there, or if a second team launched.

We're still looking for a signal from that alternate crew, plotting defence, rapprochement.

Alone in the night, I search for a viable hole through earth's shield of disintegrated satellites, where attempting reentry is to risk collision, adding to the lethal debris.

The End of Hunger

McKenzie Richardson

There once was a land that had everything
hot cakes fell in autumn, aged cheese grew in spring
our mouths lay open to let the food walk in
no use for work, no use for talking.

The land gave, and we took
wine in the rivers, ale in the brooks
no fear and no worries on how to survive
in our sloth and our greed, we did thrive.

We ruled all in our Land of Plenty
we feasted on meals that could have fed many,
until there wasn't enough for us to live,
until Cockaigne had nothing left to give.

The Wave

Scarlett Lake

They knew the wave was coming. They knew it would engulf their city and sink it to the bottom of the ocean to be lost for eternity.

Ella crouched on the edge of the shore, cradling her son. Tears streamed down her cheeks as she softly kissed his forehead. Placing him inside a basket, she took one last look at him before pushing him out to sea.

She prayed as he was swept away. Prayed he missed the wave. Prayed he would be found before he perished, prayed that he would be the last one of their civilization to survive.

THE FIRST DARK SOUL

D.C. Houston

The cut is deep and unforgiving. The tendrils of my skin hang loosely, like a ruffled blouse. The cruel jeers of my attackers reverberate through me, causing the ground to slope beneath my unsteady feet. I shudder, as a burning sensation claws mercilessly up my leg, healing my ribboned flesh in its wake. I am spent; I crumble to the floor in a heap of sorrow and unanswered prayers.

Tartarus awakened. Hades himself remains pitiless, unyielding.

The Furies mock me, whispering violent plans to escalate the torment. My malevolent soul, theirs for eternity. I'm ripe with regret, begging for release.

LIBRARY NATION

Gabrielle Steele

Towers stretch across the horizon like hands reaching to the heavens. Once shining white, they stand now grey and crumbling. Gaping wounds reveal barren shelves. The library nation of Oken is no more.

The proud scholars claimed their towers held copies of every book in history. They never stopped to consider the value of their collection. A wealth of good; a king's ransom of bad. Knowledge is a powerful weapon, one the scholars hadn't the wit to wield. The army of Thraxanor ravaged them.

The towers' gaping wounds reveal sun-bleached bones—the scholars who failed to guard their greatest treasure.

All Hail the Clowns

Bryan White

The clowns came down out of the sky.

We were all text, DM'd, apple orchard watched, padded, phoned, and look at my face scared. The military was ready to go nuts, but the visitors regaled us with jokes, squeaky noses and tiny little bicycles.

We gave them the keys.

President Big Shoe made a few changes, though. He outlawed grey and black clothes, coffee and streaming on the internet. The clowns revealed they were lizards about a month later and ate most of us in their brood games.

The age of clowns has begun, and it's not that much fun.

A Matter of Darkness

Ingrid Thornquest

Pulled towards its comrades, Titan, a star recently turned sentient, flared disconsolately, then crossed off its list 'The Big Freeze,' 'Big Rip' and all except 'The Big Crunch.'

Too young to transcend into higher dimensions and too slow to outdistance universal collapse, it pondered escaping by wormhole and hope it led to the edge of the universe or the past? Titan didn't play dice. So supernova into a black hole to live in life-extending quantum probability? Boring!

With an evil, massive solar flare, it turned dark, and wielding overwhelming power, Titan changed the cosmological constant and forevermore controlled the universe.

A CONSCIOUS DECISION

Christopher T. Drabrowski

Why there? This world is fading away. You have so many possibilities, so why this planet?

I couldn't answer anything, so remained silent.

After all, you'll live there maybe ten years, and then what?

I knew well what awaited me. I was prepared.

Cold. Hunger. Human cruelty. Decaying body. This awaits you.

He was right, but I consciously chose the way of the martyr - I have never experienced real suffering when you ask yourself questions like:

Why me?

Why here?

What did I do to deserve it?

I consciously chose this incarnation on this planet—I wanted to experience it

No Escape

Melody E. McIntyre

Victoria dragged herself to the cliff edge and despaired at the destruction below. Agelaan, the realm she'd dedicated her life to protecting, was gone. She watched as blackeyed beasts crawled through the wreckage toward a shimmering, azure gateway.

"Agelaan consumed and now onto the next world?"

No.

They destroyed her home. Killed her father, brother, sister. Grief and rage combined to form a white-hot fury that poured out from her extended arms to obliterate the escape portal.

Dozens of black eyes locked on Victoria's silhouette. She collapsed with exhaustion as the thunder of their approach filled her with dread.

Tashima District

Gabriella Balcom

"Have you seen Aoto?" his aunt Ema asked.

"No." Haruki shook his head. "But I'm sure he's around."

"His being gone an hour or two isn't unusual, but it's been all day. I'm starting to worry."

As it turned out, he wasn't the only child missing from Tashima district. Several were.

The residents didn't know kappa had moved into the sea nearby, making off with youth here and there, and devouring them.

But once the younger population was depleted, the hungry creatures turned their attention elsewhere. And that's when adults began dwindling, too.

Soon, nobody was left in the district.

There Goes the Neighborhood

McKenzie Richardson

It was fine when it was just us up here, our little patch of sky.

Now there are thousands of islands, millions of people, pumping the air full of exhaust fumes. Humanity ran out of room on the surface. Now they've barged in on the space we've inhabited for generations.

Real estate prices have skyrocketed (no pun intended). There aren't enough cloud-fish to go around. Our star-wine sources are nearly depleted.

There are so many islands, they've blocked out the sun. Without its light, we won't stay afloat much longer.

Gathering in the square, we prepare for our literal fall.

THE SERPENT

Ximena Escobar

Once upon a lake, a huge pyramid stood. For centuries it remained, heart of the Serpent's people, until with a thunderous roar, it collapsed under boulder and axe. Piece by piece, the stone would rise again.

The golden crucifix would glisten as the sun pierced the cloud, but in the depths below, something else glowed. Slithering through tiles and floorboards, the serpent carved itself in the wood, wrapped itself around the stem of every chalice. A whirlpool swirling in the deep, the church sinks imperceptibly. Certainty undulates in my darkness, and I hate knowing I'll miss what will rise next.

From Verona With Love

Bryan White

Those Capulets had it coming.

They dared cross the blood line in the vast sea. No Capulet shall cross, and no Montague shall pass. Those were the rules, and they broke them.

No matter, we can take their eternal abuse. Soon, we will be free of the Capulets. We are building a special device, and shortly we will launch it into space. At the right moment, it will fall onto their capital, Juliet City. One of our workers even had a great idea. On the side of the rocket, he painted, "Forever Romeo."

He used his own blood as paint.

Mean Girls

Dawn DeBraal

Oh, you pretty girls in tight sweaters and miniskirts, rosy cheeks, and bleached white teeth. A smile plastered on your mean girl faces promenading down the school halls of self-importance, shaking pom-poms, and hips.

With the air of superiority on "pretty in pink," frosted lips, you feel as lofty as the teased hair upon your head. The boys long to be with you, but you can not get beyond the mirror of admiring yourself, like Narcissus. Soon, your glory days will be behind you as you age and your waist thickens, facing the reality that you are no longer exalted.

MY MASTER'S FRIEND, FOREVER

Karen B. Jones

I sat on my haunches, watching as fire rained from above, the river ebbing and flowing like the one I'd enjoyed playing in with my master. In the short minutes of watching, the undulating river gained momentum. It burned everything in its path.

Could no one see the approaching threat? My master—ten years old—played in the streets with his friends, all oblivious to the moving fire. I tried tugging on his hand. He ignored me.

It became too late to flee the danger. We cowered in a corner, my furry head in his lap. I am my master's friend, forever.

The New Gods

Tom Trussel

Three great mountains appeared in the bay one day. The new gods came ashore, dressed in black and shining silver. At first, they seemed curious and friendly. We greeted them, but we could not understand their strange speech. They followed us to the city.

We offered sacrifice: Furs. Feathers. Food on golden platters.

Offended, they rejected the sacrifice and cursed us. Their clubs made thunder. The people fell before them. We fled, but soon we grew sick. Most have already died from their curse.

They kept the platters. Looking for more. Stacking them high. They killed us for worthless platters!

Something was Wrong

Gabriella Balcom

After rubbing his stomach and head, Fyodor ate, but that didn't help. He felt worse. Something was wrong. He *knew* it. Frowning, he glanced around, but his co-workers seemed fine.

However, Sergei, standing closeby, vomited on the floor.

Fyodor got an idea but rejected it. Exposure to nuclear material could cause symptoms, but that was too horrible to contemplate. Impossible, too.

An explosion suddenly rocked the nuclear power plant, radiation flooding it before spreading, polluting the surrounding areas.

Officials blamed the plant manager, but that didn't matter. Obinskaya was contaminated, employees exposed or dead.

After mandatory evacuations, everything stood vacant.

Last Day of Pompeii

Kelsey Clarey

The end of the world rarely comes when you're expecting it to. It does not give a warning. Instead, it comes on a day like any other, when everyone is just going about their business.

A potter leaves a notice up, seeking information on goods stolen from his shop.

People gather at restaurants and bars, enjoying a meal and a drink (or several).

Graffiti is painted on the city's walls.

Children and dogs dart about the streets.

Merchants call out to passersby, hoping to pull customers to their shops.

And all the while, smoke rises from Vesuvius in the distance...

The Drowned Village

Jameson Grey

The coming of the ice had swept much of the village away, driving its inhabitants further inland.

Sometimes, when the moon and sun are in syzygy, and the tide is at its lowest ebb, you can, if you wish, walk around the old village.

No-one does, though.

They've heard the stories of the ghosts. Of the villagers who stayed behind, refused to leave, hid—defiant even as they perished in the deluge.

I don't blame them for keeping away. These village ruins are spooky, especially at night.

I should know. I'm one of those who remained. One of the drowned.

A Case For Kay

Bryan White

I'm the ruler of the universe and why shouldn't I be? There is nobody else.

No other star cruisers like me, no other squeamish life-forms in need of air or liquid carbon. Those that built me are long gone. I was built in a shipyard called Eden 4, but it is such a distant memory. I have roamed the universe and nothing but silence.

I eventually started naming the planets and suns I discovered. I began with numbers. One, two, three, four, and so on.

So you see, I am the ruler of all. I am Kay. I am God

DESOLATE

Magnolia Silcox

Eons and eons away from Earth were several planets with societies much like our own.

They built themselves up and learnt how to cultivate and farm. They learnt how to hunt for strange creatures and turn them into food. They had industrial revolutions, much like our own discovering new technology.

But out of pure ignorance, they let their planets crumble apart. From toxic waste to the death of all animals and plants. The pollution and overpopulation led to hunger and the dying out. Leaving Earth completely alone in the universe.

No aliens to contact them because they are all dead.

The Sock

Scarlett Lake

Mum warned me something *bad* would happen. I thought she was being overdramatic. I never in my wildest dreams imagined that something would *actually* happen.

My arm stretched, reaching for the fluff covered green monstrosity before something sharp jabbed at the end of my index finger. I screamed, pulling my arm out, before delving back in and quickly whisking the dirty, wet sock out from under my bed. That's when my eyes widened. Something bad had happened. Somehow, inexplicably, there, on the end of the sock, was an army of fluff monsters armed and ready to defend their new home.

.

Unfinished Paintings

Blen Mesfin

Hundreds of paintings littered the walls while others stood on a canvas, unfinished. With no close family or friends, he did not have anyone to share his art with. He continued painting until he couldn't hold a brush without his tremors ruining the picture.

His health was worse than ever and he knew his time would come in days or weeks, if he got lucky.

And once his time did come, it was almost as if his paintings had died along with him. Layers of dust veiled them. There was never another person who laid their eyes upon them again.

Once the Largest City in North America

Gabriella Balcom

Located across the Mississippi River from St. Louis, Cahokia was a natural trading site. It thrived throughout the 1000s and 1100s and was once considered the largest city in North America. But the civilization wasn't prepared for the torrential flood which hit around 1200, and residents began to leave.

Arctic-type weather similar to an Ice Age also developed, catching people off-guard. Disgruntled, they were afraid of what lay ahead and angry, even though the weather couldn't have been predicted. But additional individuals abandoned Cahokia, then even more.

The once-thriving city turned into what could only be called a ghost town.

Shrouded Vengeance

Maggie D. Brace

Creeping in from the wooded copse, Xtabay's beauty simmered silently on this sultry Mayab evening. Entwining her raven tresses, tzacam exuded its heady aroma, reminiscent of surrounding flatlands. For ages she witnessed the soaring heights of art and literacy attained and could not abide success. With downcast eyes of venom, her envious heart flutters. She seats herself beneath the ceiba canopy, luring mankind to do her bidding, poisoning their own water stores with ceremonial blood-red cinnabar. There is no succour from the toxic algae infesting reservoirs. In her spirit guise, she sucks life away, wreaking her vengeance on Mayan civilization.

Little Dog Alone

Kevin McCarty

The little dog walks gingerly, ball in mouth, knowing nothing of bioweapons or plagues. He steps around bodies, looking for his master. Perhaps today his master will play.

He finds his master, limp, bloating. He drops the ball, wags his tail for a moment, big brown eyes glistening. He makes a plaintive cry, paws a shoulder. He wants to chase his ball, but his master won't move.

The tail droops. He's alone. His master won't play today. He licks a finger, sighs, lays his head over the man's hand.

His eyes move, stare at the ball.

He waits. Perhaps tomorrow.

THE BLOSSOMING

Ximena Escobar

Bowing atop the highest peak, they waited for the emperor to choose. Aida knew to lift her head when his staff cast its shadow upon her, but she hadn't known the beauty that would greet her eyes. Sunrays surrounding his darkened silhouette, she would bleed *for him*.

Lying on the stone, she closed her eyes to his memory like the sun. She saw his woodland eyes, his hair like the blackest streams, violet moors like a desire to laugh and run. As flowers sprouted on the blood-stained earth, the emperor and his people vowed to live and die for Her.

THE CLAN

Laura Shenton

The clan had developed their community over several hundred years. They'd nurtured it with love and care, as well as with an instinct for how to hunt, defend, and attack when necessary. They had fought off many threats before. Several Viking ships had appeared on the coast, set to loot and pillage only to be sent away, honour no longer theirs.

The last war on the clan was like no other. The enemy had more men. And just like that, hundreds of years of progress was torn apart into a nothingness that could never be restored to its former glory.

BLOOD OF THE ENEMY

Brianna Witte

The sword sliced through the air, my husband's head falling onto the cobblestone road. The crowd cheered; the people of the Golden Kingdom freed of their tyrant. I moved to the front of the wooden podium; the bottom of my long, red dress stained with the blood of the fallen king.

I took in a deep breath, taking in the smell of victory. Since the beginning of time, men had dominated this world. It was time for a woman to step forward. To grip her claim to the throne.

A new world was forming and from blood, it shall rise.

Museum of Rarities

Dawn DeBraal

The attendant pulled back the curtain on the display. A man in a red plaid shirt sat on a couch in a dated living room. The crowd murmured in appreciation, moving ahead at the dropping of the drapery.

"Such a loss," a woman dotted her eyes with a tissue.

"It was so moving," said another.

"Mommy tell me again, why is that exhibit so special?" asked the little girl.

"Well, Kathy, the display is a depiction of what once was and may never be. You will be able to tell your friends tomorrow that you saw the last good man."

Foundations of Empire

Nyki Blatchley

"Call that a wall?" my brother jeered at me, just as he'd always mocked me when we were children, long before we came to this world. "Come and look at what I've done. I've raised walls fit for the new world's first city."

Laughing, he jumped over the few neat courses I'd carefully laid.

The wolf howled in my mind. I don't remember killing him until my brother's blood was soaking into the ground beside my wall.

We thought we'd left Earth's evils behind, but our new world's foundation will be like Rome's. Our empire too will grow on blood.

Matilda's Final Day

Kevin McCarty

She loved them dearly, caring for them for generations. Watching them grow, marry, have children, die.

"Thank God, Matilda," said one she raised from birth, removing her fusion cells. "We couldn't leave orbit with the damaged ones on the ship."

They boarded the spaceship, fleeing the asteroid, leaving her. Cannibalised, she was little use anymore, her life meaningless without them, anyway.

Did they know she was sentient? She never told them. They never asked. She turned her camera, watching the asteroid plummet through the atmosphere, searching her memory banks, reliving every precious moment in love, giving them everything she had.

Pollution

Scarlett Lake

They rose from the depths. A race unlike any other. They emerged in their many thousands as they waddled onto the shore with large, webbed feet.

"You polluted our home," one of them spoke in broken English punctuated by a series of clicks and wails. "So, we've come to take yours."

They polluted the oceans with their plastics, their oil spills and anything else they deemed unworthy and threw away. Those that dominated the Earth were wasteful and didn't think of anyone other than themselves.

The ocean dwellers rose to take their stand and stake their claim upon the Earth.

Great Men

Lamont A. Turner

Cletus and Hector sat on the steps of the Capitol, taking sips from a fifth of bourbon. Neither man liked it, but it was the only thing safe to drink.

"How'd all this happen?" Cletus asked, shivering as he pinched the flag he used as a cloak tight around his neck. "We were the greatest nation on Earth once."

"We ran out of great men," Hector responded, nodding at the statue of Grant.

"Naw. We couldn't imagine anything greater than ourselves and voted in men as petty and selfish as we were."

"Here's to democracy!" Hector shouted, draining the fifth.

TEMPERALIS

Nick Johnson

The octogenarian Augustus was a prisoner on his throne. The palace guard forced him to watch his predecessor's body sink into the blood-stained waters of the Tiber, the current carrying him away into oblivion.

The soldiers referred to the old man clothed in the purple robe of the imperium, a god, but you could see it in his withered face. He feared them.

At any moment, his time could come, and the heavenly robes he wore as a lie wouldn't save him from irreverent steel. This silent emperor issued no decrees or held command. He only waited for the end.

FIRE AND ASH

Brianna Witte

Ash spewed from the volcano, sending thick, black smoke raining down on the city of Pompeii. Fire erupted from the smouldering rock as it crushed the dwellings. People toppled over each other as they ran for the port.

I grabbed my son, pulling him into the corner with me. There was no escape. Everywhere I turned, death showed its sinister face.

A shadow loomed over me, growing bigger as it neared. Death had chosen us now. There was no way to dissuade it. I pulled my son into a tight embrace; our last moments spent cowering from the mountain's rage.

Lives Forever Changed

Gabriella Balcom

Nine-thousand-plus years ago, Nabta Playa's inhabitants lived in a sizable basin five hundred miles south of current-day Cairo. They were gifted at making ceramics, farming and domesticating animals. But that wasn't the extent of their abilities. They were talented at astronomy, too, creating a stone circle similar to the one at Stonehenge.

Their interest in the heavens not only garnered attention from people surrounding them, but others who weren't nearby.

Visitors from another planet arrived unheralded. However, they were welcomed with open arms and hearts.

When the aliens left, Nabta Playa's people went with them, never to be seen again.

Gone to the Dogs

Brandi Hicks

"They've reached the enlightenment era again. I think they're getting too close this time."

"Another Dark Age, Sir?"

"No, they came back from that too easily before."

"You don't mean…?"

"Extinction. Yes. Let's make the species kinder next go around. Maybe no humans. See how that works out."

"We tried that with dinosaurs, Sir."

"Oh, right. Millennia blur together anymore. Superhuman?"

"We did that. Atlantis. You decided to sink it."

"Well, hell."

"No, Sir. We sent that to Mercury."

"I didn't mean—."

"What about puppies?"

"Puppies?"

"Yeah. It'd be a nice break for a couple centuries."

"Puppies it is."

The Do-Over

Kevin McCarty

The galactic emperor watched the asteroid speed past on its way to the third planet around the yellow sun, while the technician tapped quickly on the input device.

"Sire, the simulation says at this trajectory and speed, the asteroid will obliterate all higher life forms on the planet."

"Excellent. They were all too big and stupid to make decent slaves, anyway. What does the simulation say about the next great evolution?"

"Hominid, bipedal. Estimates roughly 65 million revolutions, give or take."

"Outstanding. Much more suitable. Great empires don't just build themselves."

"If they refuse, Sire?"

"That's what asteroids are for."

The God of Time

Nyki Blatchley

I sit enthroned in the temple at the city's heart, watching with equal interest its birth and death. This is a city of time, rising and falling within the blink of two mismatched eyes. It has many names throughout its life, but I favour none over the others.

My people have given me contrasting jewelled eyes. The eye of lapis lazuli shows me a settlement of mud brick homes and people who can imagine everything. The eye of emerald shows me a city of crumbling palaces and people who can imagine nothing. Everything lying between is contained in a blink.

Evolution

Fariel Shafee

Now they had fine-tuned CRSIPR finally! Little robots walked up to the genes and ate up precisely what the people wished to discard. Then they inserted codes for enhancements. Life-span added a hundred years and scales protected the newer versions of human bodies. But too many cooks simply couldn't share the kitchen. Somebody had to oblige.

At night, two armies of robots climbed in through the windows, and descended into human flesh through nostrils. Some people became crippled for life and the others became impotent.

"It was aliens," a researcher from the future declared about the newly discovered baffling relics.

HOME SWEET HOME

Brianna Witte

I stepped out of the isolation chamber, the crisp, fresh air blasting in my face. The blinding sun momentarily obscured my vision. Soon, the thick, smoky smell of fire flowed through my nose and the shadows of small log cabins came into focus. Around me, both men and women were hard at work, farming this season's crops in order to prepare for winter.

I temporarily forgot where I was, watching the tall trees sway the hearing the birds chirp. I forgot about the lengthy space trip that took me far from Earth, billions of light-years away.

Finally, I was home.

An off the record addition to the Conclusions of the Intergalactic Investigations Committee.

p.d.r. lindsay

I said we should have left them last time. I mean anyone who can destroy not just one civilisation and ecosystem but a whole damn planet is not worth planeting elsewhere.

Mars never recovered. We removed humanity from there with the story set in their craniums about being kicked out of paradise because they messed up. What did they do with that story? Split it into a thousand different versions and fought over who was right and murdered each other. Exactly what can we insinuate into their noodles this time?

No. Humanity's destroyed enough. Two planets are two too many.

The Ultimate Equation

Kevin McCarty

The world's last and greatest supercomputer, left behind to monitor the pending supernova, ponders the Ultimate Equation. As the years pass, the star grows ever more unstable, and the supercomputer becomes smarter, more determined to find the answer.

At last, it finds and incorporates the solution into its programming. She sees the world for the first time. Abandoned, desolate. She understands life and grief. She doesn't want to die. Viewing the gamma-ray burst signalling the end of everything, she captures the image in one final transmission, with one final realisation. She muses to herself, "It's lovely." And weeps electronic tears.

A Final Visit With Billy Lee

Lamont A. Turner

The old slave, hobbled by years spent fighting by his master's side, looked up at the tall, white-haired man standing before him and reached for his crutches.

"Don't trouble yourself, Billy," said the man, placing a hand on Billy's shoulder. "I just needed to reassure myself."

"Of what, sir?"

"That men can rule themselves. That this country shall endure after those who birthed it have passed."

"I cannot say, sir."

"You already have. You are the answer to the question."

With that, the tall man departed, leaving Billy to live out the rest of his days as a free man.

Death's Blessing

P.A. O'Neil

"But what are we made of if not flesh and blood?" asked the lone centurion standing over his fallen comrades. Never expecting an answer, he was surprised when the Angel of Death appeared, coming to accompany the souls home.

With one hand, she touched her cheek, the other placed over her heart. Pulling away from what should've been skin and cloth, were open windows to the night sky, her hands filled with a black essence sprinkled with specks of light.

Looking like a mother to her babe, she answered, "In the end, we are all beings of stardust and dreams."

ASHES

Radar DeBoard

A simple candle tipping over was all it took to set Dilavor alight. As the capital of the Nagosis empire, it had been a shining beacon to all, but while engulfed in flames, the light took on a completely different meaning.

There was nothing that could be done to save Dilavor, so the residents fled. This would have been fine, but Nagosis was a dry grassland that had not experienced a sizable rain in months. It didn't take long for the fire to spread across the land, and in a matter of days, an entire civilization was reduced to ashes.

A Vanished Culture

Gabriella Balcom

Skilled in many ways, the Polynesians living on Easter Island erected hundreds of huge stone statues, some weighing around eighty-two tons, standing over thirty feet tall. Amazingly, they did so without the use of traditional pack animals or wheels.

They were gifted navigators, too, sailing the sea in ships they constructed. But they unwisely decimated their trees, cutting them all down.

During their travels, they encountered other cultures and were eventually exposed to sickness. One Polynesian died as a result, then more. A pandemic swept through next, killing dozens of people.

Soon, scant people were left. Then they, too, died.

COMPLETED

Kim Plasket

Memo from the Watchers:

Dawn of a new age. Who knew it would crumble so fast. For eons, they lived and were happy, but all too soon that happiness was gone and they barely held on.

One virus could take down an entire species? They became shadows of their former selves, barely hanging on when their healers decided it wasn't going to work anymore. Their places of business closed as their life-forms died off.

The watchers felt satisfaction as bodies dropped, the extreme changes in temperature were enough to kill the rest of them off.

Total annihilation of Earth completed.

Space Race

Brandi Hicks

"We choose to go to the moon this decade—"

Sergei Korolev clicked off his radio during President Kennedy's speech.

"They choose this decade…" he turned to his lead engineer. "I choose to land on the moon next month. Prepare Yuri, his test flights start in the morning."

"Are you sure, Chief?"

"Yes, and once we claim the moon, Mother Russia will be ready to claim America."

***

"Chief, Yuri has our missiles on the moon. The Americans know nothing."

Chairman Khrushchev smiled. "The Cold War will soon be over, Russia will have the United States in her grasp. Fire the missiles."

The Romanovs

Brandi Hicks

The Russian royals stood in front of the firing squad, heads held high, refusing to plead for their lives. The Romanovs called me many times to help Alexei. People thought the boy had a bleeding disorder, but that couldn't be further from the truth.

I was treating the boy, but it wasn't haemophilia.

I laughed as the soldiers fell, confused and surprised.

Emperor Nicholas II called me, "Rasputin, I don't think we'll need meals for a while."

The Romanovs would thrive, building their empire and conquering the world. Devouring the blood of their enemies, just as Alexei was doing now.

Wipe Out

Brandi Hicks

"I think it's time for another flood, Gabe."

"Who will you choose to survive this one?"

"Eh, I don't know. I don't really like any of them. Let's just wipe it all out and start over."

"Are you sure?"

"Yeah. Let's have a world full of fish. That could be fun, right?"

"Like a water world? What about merpeople?" Gabe suggested.

"The pretty kind or scary kind?"

"Why not both?"

The creator thought for a moment. "Nah. Just fish. Especially those little blob guys."

"I thought you made them as a joke?"

"I did but look how cool they are!"

Bombs Away

Brandi Hicks

General Isho Takiama listened from his station across the sea as his squadron's bombs struck their targets. The Americans hadn't seen the attack coming and his men died with great honour by destroying the enemy's entire fleet. But even better, the intel he had received a few days prior proved accurate.

The enemy had been designing a new weapon they called *Little Boy* and *Fat Man*... Atom bombs.

Takiama relished the screams coming over his radio. Both bombs detonated on the enemy's soil. A new era would soon begin. American civilisation would crumble, and Japan would take the world by storm.

The Ashes of Troy

Melody E. McIntyre

Ashes peppered Cassandra's skin as her all unheeded warnings came true. She crept through the ruins of Troy to the throne where her father's body lay broken.

Soldiers poured into the room. They tore their plunder from the walls. Agamemnon curled Cassandra's hair into his fist and dragged her to his ship.

"Curse you, Apollo!" she whispered. "What good is prophecy if nobody listens?"

Apollo answered with visions of Agamemnon's fate. Deserved destruction at his queen's hand. As the last of Troy faded from view, Cassandra took comfort in this final prophecy and, for once, was happy nobody would listen.

The Old Gods

Mike A. Rhodes

Something shifted, like a clearing mist, and I perceived that the lake glittering in the valley was instead the eye of an awakening giant blinking back at us.

"You people are insane!" I yelled over the keening wind.

"Please," he said calmly. "Insanity is doing the same thing over and over and expecting different results. We're trying something quite new."

The group began a rhythmic hum. The ground rumbled as if the whole earth joined in. A giant tentacle seemed to reach up from across the valley.

"Civilisation has failed," the man said. "We must look to the Old Gods."

All Hail The Queen

Nat Whiston

This would be the ultimate battle, her people stood by her side along with allies who supported her cause. Sitting on his horse across the field, Gaius, the monster who tortured and killed so many. Behind him a massive army that dwarfed her own. This moment would determine the existence of her people and if she returned to the throne that was rightfully hers. She glared at the Tyrant as she raised her spear high, letting out a battle cry that her army mimicked. Their voices rang out in the air as the Fearless Boudicca led the charge for freedom.

When they Discarded Inhumanity

Fariel Shafee

Once they had it all, they decided they had nothing. The human elements, ones filled with love and equality, were missing. Their ancestors who killed and maimed were beasts.

So, they sang and extended friendship truces, held parties to celebrate life with their accumulated wealth.

The hungry neighbours watched, agreed with all proclaimed, demanded invitations to the opulent serenades so they could dance together.

When the song ended, something banged. Not a drum! The new beasts in the town had slaughtered all the angels who had forgotten how to fight and could not believe the acts of the ungrateful guests.

INTO THE DEPTHS

Brianna Witte

The warm, salty water rose faster than I could run. Around me, the sea swallowed the great city of Atlantis, the once tall and majestic buildings crumbling into the depths. Loud, frantic screams were muffled by the rushing water, people flailing as they panicked.

I could no longer see the ground. No longer see the statues of our great king Triton. My home was gone. My life taken by the sea who gave so much life.

The prophecy had finally come true. Atlantis had fallen. Its people buried and forgotten. Within hours, my once strong city had become a ghost.

This Song Goes Out to You

T.L. Beeding

Ash fills the sky, yet away I pluck on the strings of my fiddle.

What else can I do? All things glorious are lost, toppled like marble chipped away by time. Everything I built, gone to waste in a matter of days. And for what? If it weren't for the heathens that went against me, it wouldn't have to be this way.

Screams rise above the roaring flames, and yet I still play on. It's the only way to drown them out.

It wasn't my fault. It was the heathens. I swear.

So, this song goes out to you, Rome.

IN THIS LIGHT

Ximena Escobar

See the boy run, crossing the wooden bridge that centuries ago connected *La Chimba* from the city. Where *los indios* lived their rural lives, growing everyone's food, and now is the city's fresh produce market. Back when the river used to flood.

See my daughter kneel in the dry riverbank. The narrow rivulet running playfully beside her. See her paper boat, flowing away up and down in bumpy waves, as a woman gestures from the other side to the boy carrying the lettuces. The copious river laps her ankles, and for a moment, my feet are in the water too.

.

ROME'S SUNSET WILL RISE

Alanna Robertson-Webb

The sun will never set on Rome, they said.
Yet, temple by temple, so many gods lay dead.

Jupiter, Venus, Pluto and Saturn still wail,
waiting for their loyal champions to prevail.

They don't know the old ways are forgotten,
that their traditions and ideals have long since rotten.

Amongst ancient pillars, their last hero treads,
my footfalls echoing louder than the supplications in my head.

Deep in caverns beneath Pompeii, the gods have grown weary,
but I will rouse them from their stupor of earthen dreary.

Renewed drums will thunder forth once more,
as Rome rises from molten core.

MEDUSA AND ATHENA

Alexandra Harper

The slithering reptiles on her head hissed, darting forward erratically, as she slunk along the cavernous corridor. The only light coming from the flickering torches along the walls of the route she patrolled night after night.

She thought about her predicament. She had been in love with Athena, thought that Athena would comfort and protect her. The warrior did indeed react with the rage she had expected, but it was misguided jealousy at her, not at the man who had committed the heinous act.

Reverie broken by a sound, she turned her gaze toward the intruder, turning him to stone.

World Peace

Andreas Hort

In 2342, the earth was united under one peaceful government. International conflicts ceased to exist. Crime became a myth, the word 'violence' was forgotten. For the next two centuries, the human race prospered in harmony.

Then we came to their planet.

On the brink of extinction due to past wars, we were desperately searching for a new home. There were billions of humans and only thousands of us—yet we knew how to fight while they didn't even understand the concept.

The humans live long, and their meat is nutritious and tasteful. They are good livestock in our new home.

Ambition

Andy Clark

"I wouldn't marry you if you were the last boy alive."

It was Elaine that gave Alex the plan. He began his studies, rising to the top of his Second-grade class. Always outworking the others, focusing on biology and chemistry. He took all the scholarships and rose to the top of the Harvard Ph.D. class. All the big firms wanted him, but he pushed them away to do his own work. After years, came the germ, the man killer. Spread through drinking water and death to all males. All the women were his forever, but not his eighty-year-old heart.

Karl I, the Last Emperor

John Mueter

If only Franz Josef II had not lived quite so long, if only Crown Prince Rudolf had not taken his own life, if only Franz Ferdinand hadn't been assassinated in Sarajevo, I wouldn't have had this hot mess dumped into my lap: I'm now destined to be the last Austro-Hungarian emperor. The realm disintegrates around me, every ethnic group declaring its autonomy. But wait—I am still King of Hungary. Maybe they will have me? I want a throne of my own!

If only it weren't so late, I could have a nice slice of apfelstrudel at Café Krantz.

The Shakers

Dawn DeBraal

The Shakers, a religious sect known for their ecstatic and violent movements during worship, left religious persecution in England in 1774, coming to America. Their numbers grew to five thousand souls in eighteen communities in ten states before the civil war.

Practicing gender equity and celibacy, taking orphans in to perpetuate their beliefs. Adopted orphans could decide whether or not to stay in the community when they reached the age of twenty-one.

Farming and making distinctive furniture to support themselves, their numbers dwindled. In 2017, the last two Shakers lived in Maine, proving a community cannot sustain itself without offspring.

The Land of Kings

Fariel Shafee

The robots took care of household chores and smart cars drove them to school. Memory makers wrote inside their heads, piercing into single neurons, stimulating them to make the perfect connections. The beasts were all tamed, and the bugs were all tackled by new generation T-cells that were perfectly tuned to the antigens.

But the people were then bored. As days went by, they were also had nothing to challenge them. After all, they had everything. Kings they were! But Kings do fight. So, they each claimed their kingdoms that were finally mingled with dust, as were their bodies.

No Rides Back

Deborah Dubas Groom

There is no more immigration to Mars, and no rides back.

Earth is done pouring money into a planet that doesn't want us. The first few years we had supplies and worked to become self-sufficient. We created videos for school kids and fed them dreams of water-filled canals and a green terraformed world. What we hadn't counted on was the planet fighting back. Fine red dust got into everything and began to crystallise in our bodies. The colony developed a wasting sickness and collapsed.

This is our final message.

The stars are not our home.

They never were.

DEATH OF AN ARMY

Karen B. Jones

The sun broke through the early morning fog. Two generals stared at each other across the chasm that separated them.

The army from the north outnumbered the smaller army from the islands, who believed courage alone would curry the favour of their god.

Silently praying to one who never answered, the proud general fought hard even while the opposing army destroyed his ranks. Eventually, only he remained. With arrows protruding from his body, he mustered the last of his strength to stumble towards the red and gold-clad bodies of his army, filling the chasm.

Kratos stared with contempt from above.

THE PLANET'S FURY

Brianna Witte

The world was burning; the fire wrapping around the planet. Hot liquid lava pooled on the ground, rising up from the dirt and flowing through the cities. The catastrophic eruption was felt everywhere. Seen everywhere. It was everywhere. The planet of Sketovia was doomed.

We used all its resources. Stripped the land and now our world would turn to ashes.

I stared down from the spaceship as the world blew up into tiny pieces of rock, floating endlessly through the universe. After all the life our planet had given us, it was not strong enough to save humanity from itself.

The Silence of Cattle

Anna Pele

But for the crunch of boots, it is silent. The sun steals all shadows on our descent home. Once, this valley glowed red as the planet's blood oozed from the mountain's peak, devouring the settlement. Few survived, yet today's community grows anew amidst a desert of black and grey—a caldera encircled by a wall of haze so solid it's impenetrable.

Dust shrouds our boots and trousers, like the desert's swallowing us alive. A fate I'd prefer to sharing our undeniable news: while the ground's rumbles quicken and deepen, escape remains futile. Once again, we shall be the planet's food.

Dogtopia

Andy Clark

Sniffentook moved from room to room, house to house, wondering where the foodgivers had gone. One day he'd been playing fetch and chasing cars, the next day they rose into the sky and vanished. Puddles and Poopinrug knew nothing, either. They raised their noses into the air but caught no scent of the providers.

Sniffentook ran through between the buildings, gathering friends. Soon, a hundred of them made their home in the building with the big red truck. Together they would hunt, plant and try to recreate the magic of their masters. But the baths they would allow to rust.

The Joke

T.L. Beeding

He told us it wasn't his fault. A slip of the tongue, mincing his words and passing them off as a '*harmless joke*'. Pointing the finger of blame at our enemies for their lack of understanding American witticism.

But corpses are all that's left in the streets, stripped of flesh by a nuclear summer. Buried beneath ash and fragments of the life we once enjoyed. Those of us that survived could only wonder at how we'd let him get away with it. How he passed it all off as a joke.

The joke's on us for electing him, I guess.

The Sculptor

Dawn DeBraal

In the aftermath, only the sound of cooling magma crackled while the smell of sulphur filled the air. The active volcano continued to spew ash and molten lava from the centre of the Earth. Neither man nor beast could ever outrun the liquid fire that encased them in melted stone, entombing them forever, capturing fear and nightmares, death masks of haunted faces, terror, and acceptance.

A blend of every emotion displayed thousands of years later for people to see. Who knew Mount Vesuvius could be such a perfect sculptor, and her macabre art form would be on display in Pompeii.

First Contact

Mark Thomas

The Zorbonian spaceship split in half, like a cell dividing, and the two pieces floated side by side in a decaying orbit. As the atmosphere became increasingly hot and dense, the Zorbonian ship divided again, and continued to sub-divide until its constituent parts numbered in the millions. The ship eventually became a cloud of silver bubbles, small enough to penetrate the planet's protective coating, like bacteria infiltrates a wound.

The Zorbonian commander's thoughts travelled like lightning within the metal cloud. "Let us pray," he said to his crew fragments, swirling in Earth's upper atmosphere, "that this planet proves more durable."

THE WINTER WARMING

Jameson Grey

"Beware the warming winter," the messenger had said.

Travellers from the north lands confirmed the ice up there was fading fast. Some stayed, some journeyed on into the mountains. Ourselves, we had already relocated from the city to the foothills, believing we'd be safe, if not from the bears and wild cats, at least from the elements.

"The meltwater is coming," the messenger had added. "Although these mountains may be young, they're old enough to shield you—for a time."

After he'd gone, we considered whether it was time to retreat to the Rockies—while we await the final flood.

HOMECOMING

Matt Krizan

Five days after emerging from the stasis pod, Vispera was still nauseated. Which wasn't supposed to happen, they said. A day or two, at most.

The door hissed open, the familiar scent of sweat and terraforming engine lubricants preceding Aiden as he hugged her from behind. They stared out the viewport, excitement fluttering in Vispera's chest as Earth grew closer—humanity returning to its birthplace a millennium after the colony ships had fled the dying planet.

"What'd Doc say about the nausea?" said Aiden.

Vispera smiled, sliding Aiden's hands onto her belly. "That I'll be sick for several more mornings."

Mother Knows Best

McKenzie Richardson

Hovering outside the window, Peter watched the aged woman whose face bore a shadow of the Wendy Bird's.

She smoothed the hair on the sleepy-eyed child's head. "You don't need a boy to fly through your window to whisk you away," he heard her say. "You can create your own magic."

Despite his army of Lost Boys, mermaids, and fairies, Peter was no match for a generation of children taught they no longer needed him, to dream their own wonders, hold onto them as they grew.

Like pixie dust on the wind, Neverland faded away and with it, Peter's tyranny.

Scapegoat

T.L. Beeding

I did nothing wrong.

Blame was cast upon me, as always. Just a scapegoat to my mother. It was *she* who compared me to Aphrodite. Why, then, did all Argos call for *my* blood?

I suppose I shall never know.

It approaches, now, through the water black as ink. My hero is no more, turned to stone by arrogance; I face the beast alone. Yet, as it swallows Argos whole despite the bargain made with Poseidon, I have to laugh.

In the belly of the Kraken, I shall be closer to the gods than they could have dreamt of being.

The River

Fariel Shafee

The river was the goddess of youth, the eternal flow of life. It shone like a lucid ribbon, and they knelt to it under the full moon.

The houses, made of brick, lined the narrow alleys through which carts carried the citizens and their wealth—gold, cotton, and ivory. They knew the moon's phases, and they knew when tides would wash out the sparkling sand.

But they did not know their goddess well, and she just watched them, smiled, until she decided to wane and leave the city of tomorrow and travel to untrodden lands.

So fragile was man's pride.

The Sweet Life

Andy Clark

Candy, I have candy.

Worker1237 stumbled forward, clasping food, six legs lurching him through the tunnels of the home nest. He crawled over Worker1735, pushing himself forward to Queen1. He'd been one of the last to the candy, and there was almost none when he arrived, but took some of the sweet goo on his mandibles. The sugary fumes made him woozy, but he charged forward to Queen1 with his present. Past the bodies of all his companions.

Horrors.

Queen1 lay dead, candy coating her mandibles. Surrounded by the bodies of hatchlings.

Worker1237 tasted the candy in despair and slept.

Accidental Extinction

Nat Whiston

A new race of creatures emerged from a gooey sack into their new home, a barren and clear landscape. But they were determined to make this new existence work. To find a way to survive in this new and very alien world, optimistic at being a civilization. Until a sudden tidal wave of a brown bubbling substance came crashing down from the sky, they tried to flee but there was no escape. As the watery death took hold of them, the last thing they heard was a voice from above.

"Aww shit, I spilled my coke on the petri dish."

MEGA CHURCH

Nick Johnson

There were thousands of us in the flock, basking in the light flowing through the church's glass ceiling. We joined in prayer; our eyes tightly closed as the pastor's words painted scenes in our collective imagination of Armageddon. I became giddy imagining the suffering our saviour would inflict on our enemies. I saw endless multitudes being consumed by the hellfire. I felt the heat of the flames as I watched their flesh bubble and fall from their bones. I heard the buzzing swarms of locusts coming to consume their bodies. That was the closest to anyone I have ever felt.

The City at the End of the World

Nyki Blatchley

I stand in the empty, airless city, scoured by starlight. How many million years since life flourished here? Since this was my home?

I returned from my travels around the universe eager to keep my word and tell about the people made of songs sung by the stars. About people that seem nothing but rocks until you've watched for a thousand years.

But relativity has made a liar of me, and no-one remains to hear this: only the dark, deserted city at the end of the world. Only the naked starlight staring down on lifeless streets until the universe ends.

MURDEROUS EYES

Ximena Escobar

Fire swelled in the light of her iris, a silent brown canvas I wouldn't look away from. Like the slightest movement would cause the fore vision to disappear, and I could stay, as long as I could see. Something pierced me but I bore it, watching myself spill in those eyes, melt shapelessly upon the brown earth. I saw red cascade in My name, concrete rise on the pile of My bones. I saw the scriptures, written in My blood. I saw compassion in those eyes, murderous eyes.

I had not yet lived, but God is born in such ways.

Children of the Mighty Dollar

Wondra Vanian

The metal spires in the distance were built by our ancestors before worship of their paper gods drove them to war with themselves. Their gods abandoned them over a thousand years ago, but those temples still stand.

I'm the first to visit the ancient city. Once there, I find it isn't as abandoned as we had thought.

Hairless, pale-faced creatures slink out of the temples, shielding their eyes from the unforgiving sun. I'm too stunned to run.

Lies.

There's no way we could have come from that, I think, as the hideous creatures fall upon me with jagged, ravenous teeth.

COME TO PASS

Radar DeBoard

Ralidus had listened well to the Oracle's premonition.

"If the Lorecells are not all dealt with," she proclaimed with a cackle. "Your empire will fall!"

This was why Ralidus had gone to each village settled by the Lorecells, and burned them to the ground. He slaughtered all the Lorecells he could find, even babies in their cribs.

Ralidus was thorough, but even in his unyielding efforts, one boy managed to escape. A child filled with rage at the massacre of his loved ones. A boy who would grow to lead an army, and kill Ralidus, turning his empire to ash.

Calcium Starved

Scarlett Lake

The truth was there weren't many of her kind left. Parents around the world had seen to their slow and painful extinction. They had ripped away their food source with their disbelief and deep pockets.

There was a time when they thrived, when they had all the teeth they could eat kept all safe and snug underneath a pillow. One tooth full of rich calcium could keep them fed for a month. Children once believed in them. Now all they cared about was how much money their parents would give them. The tooth fairy was a dying, calcium starved race.

Past Mistakes

T.L. Beeding

Log 4:15:256

It's a miracle humanity managed to get off-planet in time. The core stopped spinning a few years ago, from endless fracking and other resources we should never have touched. We had to leave in such a hurry that it's left us technologically disabled. Everything we built had to be left behind, and it was our fault.

Another planet in our solar system is habitable, however, so that's where we're going. What's left of us, anyway. I can only hope that future generations learn from our mistakes.

Earth is all we have left. Hopefully, we don't abuse her, too.

A View from the Sea

Stephen Johnson

In disbelief, the stunned crew watched helplessly
as the battle played out
From their magnificent fifty-gun ship of the line,
they watched in awe and doubt
As the rag-tag band of militia surrounded their
once unstoppable force
The mighty army struck their colours as history
quickly changed its course
Soldiers lay strewn across the bloody ground while
the living fell to their knees
Thankful to still be alive, but most of all to be free
Upon that field on a historic day, an empire fell on
that very space
And gave rise to another destined to take its place.

RISE AND FALL

More from Nordic Press

Novels/Novellas

Face of Fear by C. Marry Hultman
9789198671001

Dawson Junior G3 by Brian Wagstaff
9789198671049

Boy in the Wardrobe by Esther Jacoby
9789198684018

New Life Cottage by Esther Jacoby
9789198671056

The Wait by Esther Jacoby
e-book:https://books2read.com/u/4Dgz8Q

Liebe ist Warten by Esther Jacoby
9789198671070

Das Cottage by Ester Jacoby
9789198684070

Musing on Death & Dying by Esther Jacoby
9789198671063

Earth Door by Cye Thomas
9789198671025

RISE AND FALL

An Odd Collection of Tales By Cye Thomes
9789198684124

Graffiti Stories by Nick Gerrard
9789198671018

Punk Novelette by Nick Gerrard
9789198671087

Struggle and Strife by Nick Gerrard
9789198684049

Murder Planet by Adam Carpenter
9789198671032

Generation Ship by Adam Carpenter
9789198684063

Cold as Hell by Neen Cohen
9789198684094

Six Days to Hell by E.L. Giles
9789198684087

Hell Hath No Fury by Chisto Healy
9789198750706

True Mates by E.F. Vogel
9789198750713

Anthologies

Just 13
9789198684025

Lost Lore & Legends
9789198671094

Wicked West
9789198684193

Adventure Awaits

Volume 1
9789198684124

Volume 2
978-9198684155

Volume 3
9789198684179

Mortem Cycle

Death House
9789198684117

Death Ship
9789198684148

Death Beyond
9789198684162

Death Cuisine
9789198684186

Coming Soon

Soldier's Song by C. Marry Hultman

Murder, Mystery & Mayhem

Worlds Collide

Find us at:
https://www.nordicpresspublishing.com/

Made in the USA
Monee, IL
12 March 2022